Dear Parent:
Your child's love of reading starts here!

Every child learns to read in a different way and at his or her own speed. You can help your young reader improve and become more confident by encouraging his or her own interests and abilities. You can also guide your child's spiritual development by reading stories with biblical values and Bible stories, like I Can Read! books published by Zonderkidz. From books your child reads with you to the first books he or she reads alone, there are I Can Read! books for every stage of reading:

SHARED READING
Basic language, word repetition, and whimsical illustrations, ideal for sharing with your emergent reader.

BEGINNING READING
Short sentences, familiar words, and simple concepts for children eager to read on their own.

READING WITH HELP
Engaging stories, longer sentences, and language play for developing readers.

READING ALONE
Complex plots, challenging vocabulary, and high-interest topics for the independent reader.

ADVANCED READING
Short paragraphs, chapters, and exciting themes for the perfect bridge to chapter books.

I Can Read! books have introduced children to the joy of reading since 1957. Featuring award-winning authors and illustrators and a fabulous cast of beloved characters, I Can Read! books set the standard for beginning readers.

A lifetime of discovery begins with the magical words **"I Can Read!"**

Visit www.icanread.com for information on enriching your child's reading experience.
Visit www.zonderkidz.com for more Zonderkidz I Can Read! titles.

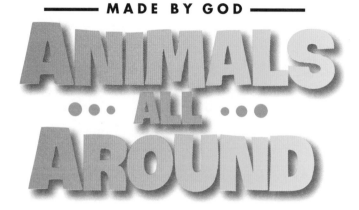

— MADE BY GOD —

ANIMALS
... ALL ...
AROUND

ZONDERKIDZ

Animals All Around
Copyright © 2013 ZonderKidz

Requests for information should be addressed to:

Zonderkidz, 5300 Patterson Ave SE, Grand Rapids, Michigan 49530

Library of Congress Cataloging-in-Publication Data

Animals all around : forest friends, our feathered friends, cats, dogs, hamsters, and
    horses, barnyard critters.
            pages   cm.
        "Made by God animals all around."
        ISBN 978-0-310-73125-2 (hardcover)
        [1. Animals—Juvenile literature.]
    QL49.A587363   2014
    590— dc23   2013029398

Editor: Mary Hassinger
Design: Cindy Davis

Printed in China

13 14 15 16 /DSC/ 22 21 20 19 18 17 16 15 14 13 12 11 10 9 8 7 6 5 4 3 2 1

TABLE OF CONTENTS

FOREST FRIENDS

Forest:
A large area of land covered with trees and other plant life.

About one-third of the land in the United States is forestland.

God created everything

and made it all good.

He made beautiful forests filled

with animals.

The forest has some small animals

and some really big ones too!

One really big forest animal is the …

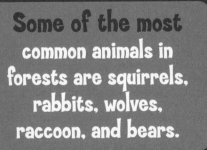

MOOSE!

Most moose in the world are found in Canada, Alaska, Scandinavia, and Russia.

Alaska and Maine have the most moose in the United States.

Moose are large mammals.

Some are seven feet tall!

That does not include their antlers.

One of the biggest racks of antlers

was over six feet wide!

A moose can weigh up to 1,500 pounds.

Moose love to eat twigs, bark, roots, and shoots of plants.

A female moose is pregnant for eight months.

Calves stay with their mom until they are one year old.

Male moose are called bulls.

Female moose are called cows.

Baby moose are called calves.

Moose have long legs that help them run fast. They can trot at a speed of 35 miles an hour.

A moose's front legs are longer than their back legs.

Moose have 32 teeth, but no upper front teeth.

Moose are very good swimmers.

They can stay underwater

for up to a minute.

Some can dive 20 feet underwater.

Some moose
can swim up to
six miles an hour!

A moose's nose
closes when he
dips his head
underwater.

Do you know another forest animal
that is a good swimmer?
It is the …

They also will go
into the water to
escape wolf packs or
even pests like flies.

PORCUPINE!

One porcupine can have as many as 30,000 quills.

When a porcupine is upset it will stomp its feet and shake its quills.

Porcupines' backs are covered with long, needle-like spines called quills.

These quills are hollow.

The quills help them float.

It is not true that porcupines shoot their quills.

Native Americans sometimes used porcupine quills to decorate clothes and bags.

Be careful around porcupines!

Their quills can grow up to a foot long.

They are very, very sharp.

Porcupines are born with soft bristles.

The bristles harden with time.

Besides being good swimmers,
porcupines can climb!
Some can climb 100 feet up trees
where they eat branches and leaves.
They also eat fruit and tender leaf and
flower buds.

Porcupines are herbivores, so while they swim they often eat water plants.

Some porcupines that live in trees hold onto branches with their tails like a monkey.

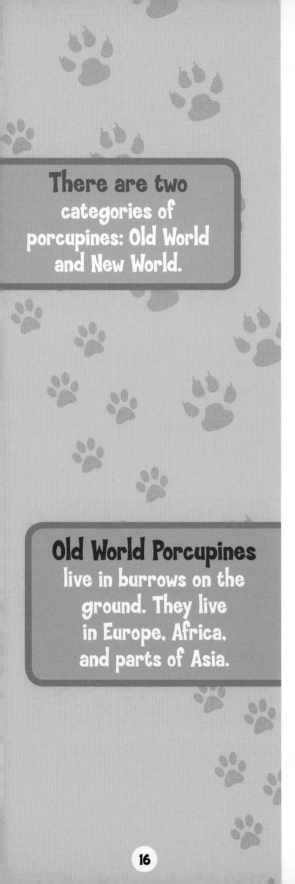

There are two categories of porcupines: Old World and New World.

Old World Porcupines live in burrows on the ground. They live in Europe, Africa, and parts of Asia.

There are 24 kinds of porcupines.

They live in North and South America, Europe, Asia, and Africa.

Porcupines live on the ground in forests, deserts, and grasslands.

Babies are called porcupettes.

New World **porcupines live up in trees.**

They live in North and South America.

Just like other rodents, porcupines have large front teeth.

This large rodent can live to be seven years old and grow to almost three feet long.

Porcupines are actually large rodents.

They are related to mice and gerbils.

Porcupines are nocturnal

like many rodents.

This means they are awake at night

and sleep during the day.

Most porcupines
like to live alone.

Porcupines are
usually ready to live
on their own when they
are about two months old.

One reason some animals are nocturnal is they live in very hot areas that make it hard to survive and find food in the heat of the day.

Another reason some animals are nocturnal is for protection from enemies that might hunt them during the day for food.

You might recognize another nocturnal animal by the rings on its tail. They are sometimes called burglars because it looks like they wear masks. It is a …

RACCOON!

Raccoons can live up to five years in the wild and live an average of 13-16 years in captivity.

A male raccoon is called a boar. A female raccoon is called a sow.

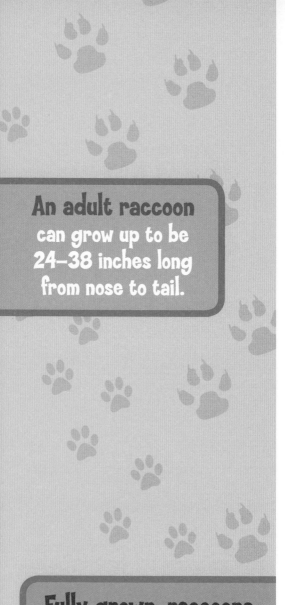

An adult raccoon can grow up to be 24–38 inches long from nose to tail.

Fully grown, raccoons can weigh 15–25 pounds, depending on the kind of food they have available.

Raccoon babies are called cubs or kits and are actually born without the black "mask."

They are curious and sneaky.

Many people see raccoons sneaking in their garbage, gardens, or yards.

Raccoons like to eat almost anything!
Their favorite foods are frogs,
mice, bugs, eggs, fruit, and garbage.
They use their paws like little hands,
holding their food just like a person.

Raccoons are amazing climbers, often hanging out in tall trees.

They also are very good swimmers, but they do not have waterproof fur, so it can be hard to move if they are soaking wet.

Raccoons do not hibernate. They might sleep for a very long time when it is cold, but they wake up easily.

Originally, raccoons were found just in North America. Now they are also found in Europe and Asia.

Raccoons live in safe places like hollow logs, caves, or small shelters, but they like warm, dry places like chimneys too!

You can see raccoons in the forest but they like to be in neighborhoods.

God made moose huge, raccoons curious,

and porcupines prickly.

He made another animal in the forest

that is very sly.

It is called a …

Moose, raccoons, and porcupines are mammals. That means they all:
- are warm blooded vertebrates.
- feed their babies with milk from their body.
- have skin that can be covered in hair.

FOX

Foxes are called "sly" which means they are clever, sneaky, and intelligent.

Foxes can use their tails as signal flags to communicate with other foxes.

Foxes are related to dogs,

but sometimes they act more like cats.

Foxes stalk their prey and play with it.

And just like a cat, they use

their tails for balance.

Some breeds of foxes are:
Arctic fox
Fennec fox
Tibetan fox
Gray fox

Some types of foxes are endangered:
Crab-eating fox
African Bat-eared fox

There are many breeds of foxes.

Some live in the forest

and are sandy, red, silver, or even black.

This breed is called the red fox.

Foxes hunt for a lot of their food.
They eat many things such as mice,
frogs, insects, birds, and rabbits.
They also like fruits and vegetables.

Most foxes like to hunt alone.

Foxes are omnivores. That means they eat meat as well as fruits and vegetables.

A mother fox can have from 2 to 12 pups at a time.

A family of pups born at the same time is called a litter.

Male foxes are called dog foxes. Female foxes are called vixen, and babies are cubs.

Just like many forest animals, foxes have become used to people and can be found in neighborhoods as well as the woods where they normally live.

Both fox parents take care of their babies until they are ready to live alone in the woods and find their own food and shelter.

Sometimes people consider foxes in their neighborhoods to be pests.

God created everything.

From the giant moose to the clever fox,

and everything in between!

The forest and our whole world

is filled with God's great creation!

OUR FEATHERED FRIENDS

Feather: structures that cover the outside of a bird's body.

Birds use their feathers for many things. Some are: protection from water, protection from cold, help in controlling flight, line and insulate nests so eggs stay warm.

God made everything,

and he made it all good.

He made bugs that crawl

under the dirt and birds that fly

way up high like the …

EAGLE!

Some types of eagles are endangered. That means they might disappear from earth!

The harpy eagle is thought to be the largest species of eagle in the world.

There are about 59 kinds of eagles.

Some kinds of eagles are:

Bald eagle

Golden eagle

African fish eagle

Steppe eagle

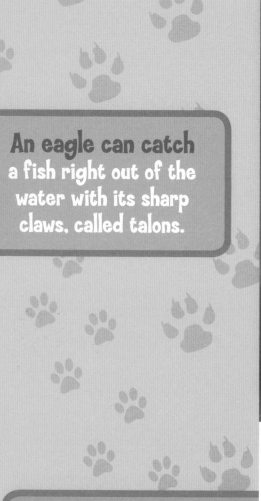

An eagle can catch a fish right out of the water with its sharp claws, called talons.

Eagle's nests can be up to 13 feet deep, and there was an eagle's nest known to weigh 1.1 tons!

Eagles are amazing birds.

Some have about 7,000 feathers!

Their wings can stretch out to be

as tall as the ceiling.

They have superstrong beaks

and claws to help them eat.

Eagles build nests of
sticks and twigs.
Some nests are huge—
up to ten feet across.
The eagles put their nests up
on cliffs or in trees to protect
their babies, called eaglets.

Baby eaglets leave their nest when they are about 12 weeks old.

Eagles usually lay two eggs at a time.

An eagle's amazing eyesight helps them see fish up to a mile away!

Eagles are carnivores. That means they eat meat.

Eagles are called birds of prey.

That means they hunt for food.

Eagles like to eat mice, snakes,

and some even like to go fishing.

God put eagles all over the world.

They like to live in high places

and near water.

One special eagle, the bald eagle,

lives in the United States

and was named the

symbol of the USA in 1782!

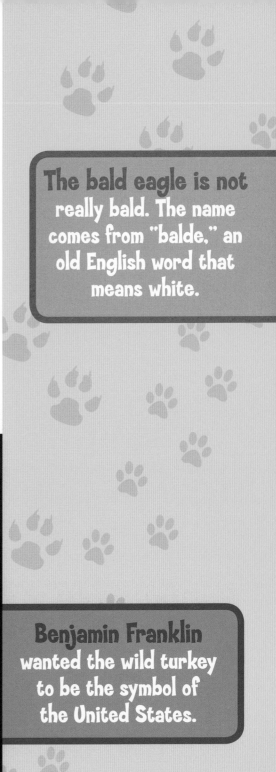

The bald eagle is not really bald. The name comes from "balde," an old English word that means white.

Benjamin Franklin wanted the wild turkey to be the symbol of the United States.

Eagles are important symbols to many Native American tribes.

The eagle is mentioned at least 30 times in the Bible.

God made the powerful eagle

and the tiny and gentle …

HUMMINGBIRD!

Despite their small size hummingbirds are one of the most aggressive bird species and will regularly attack jays, crows, and hawks that go into their territory.

Depending on the species, habitat conditions, predators, and other factors, the average wild hummingbird lives 3-12 years.

Hummingbirds migrate, which means they often fly a very long way looking for warm weather to live.

The ruby-throated hummingbird flies 500 miles nonstop across the Gulf of Mexico during both its spring and fall migrations.

The hummingbird is amazing too. There are about 320 kinds of hummingbirds. Most of them live in the western half of the world. These tiny birds love warm weather.

The smallest bird that God made
is very special.

The hummingbird's heart beats
1,260 times every minute!

Its wings beat 53 times per second.

The wings make a humming sound.

The bee hummingbird is the smallest species and measures 2.25 inches long.

A hummingbird's maximum forward flight speed is 30 miles per hour.

Hummingbirds hover by flapping their wings in a special figure-8 pattern.

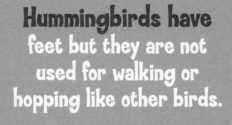
Hummingbirds have feet but they are not used for walking or hopping like other birds.

Hummingbirds can hover,

fly backward, forward,

and even upside down.

There is a long tongue in their beaks that hummingbirds use to lick at their food, up to 13-licks a second.

The bill of the sword-billed hummingbird, found in the Andes Mountains, can reach up to four inches long.

While flying, hummingbirds use a long, skinny beak to eat nectar, sap, bugs, and spiders.

A Hummingbird must consume approximately one half of its weight in sugar daily, and the average hummingbird feeds 5-8 times per hour.

Hummingbirds lay the smallest eggs of all birds. They measure less than one half inch long.

Hummingbirds are only three or four inches long.

They weigh less than one ounce.

But hummingbirds eat almost all the time.

God made these tiny, quick-flying birds, and he made the amazing and quick-running …

Hummingbirds have 1,000–1,500 feathers, the fewest number of feathers of any bird species in the world.

ROADRUNNER!

The roadrunner is New Mexico's state bird.

It is also called chaparral cock, paisano, and snake killer.

The name "roadrunner" comes from the bird's habit of racing down roads in front of moving vehicles.

Roadrunners have interesting running feet, like all cuckoo birds. It has two toes at the front and two toes at the back of its feet.

When God created the roadrunner he made them so they could run 17 miles an hour! They can fly, but they love to run.

On the roadrunner's back there is a dark patch of skin that the bird exposes to the sun to warm its body during cold weather.

A roadrunner's head has a crest of feathers like a little crown.

Roadrunners live in the desert in southwest USA and Mexico. They have a long tail that sticks straight up.

Roadrunners are part of the cuckoo bird family. Roadrunners can grow to be ten to twelve inches tall. They weigh about one-and-a-half pounds.

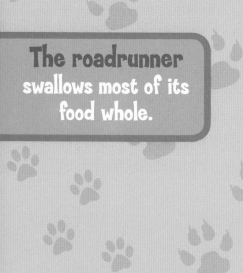

The roadrunner swallows most of its food whole.

Roadrunners can actually jump up in the air to catch a bug it wants to eat.

Roadrunners eat many things like bugs, seeds, and fruits. They can even run fast enough to catch a rattlesnake to eat it!

God made everything
and he made it all good.
He made birds that fly and
run all day,
and he made a bird that
loves the night.
It is the …

Roadrunners perform "dances" that show other birds and animals what they are feeling. For example, a male roadrunner will dance to get a female roadrunner's attention.

There are two kinds of roadrunners— the greater roadrunner and the lesser roadrunner.

OWL!

A group of owls is called a parliament, wisdom, or study. Baby owls are called owlets.

Not all owls hoot but make a wide range of other sounds such as screeches, whistles, barks, and hisses.

Owls are nocturnal.

That means they move

around the most at night.

Owl eyes work best in the dark.

Owls have superior hearing which helps them locate food even if they cannot see it.

An owl can hear a mouse stepping on a twig from 75 feet away.

A barn owl can eat up to 1,000 mice each year. Many farmers try to attract barn owls to help control rodent populations in their fields.

Owls have zygodactyl feet with two toes pointing forward and two toes pointing backward. This gives the birds a stronger, more powerful grip so they can be more effective predators.

Owls are birds of prey like the eagle.

Owls like to eat small birds and animals, bugs, and reptiles.

Owls have sharp beaks and strong claws to help them eat.

Owls can grow to be
20 to 28 inches tall.
Their wings can stretch out to be
four to five feet across.
Owls cannot move their eyes.
They turn their heads
all the way around to see!
They have special
feathers that help make them
silent when they fly.

Owls are carnivorous.

For most owl species, females are larger, heavier, and more aggressive than males.

Only 19 owl species are found in North America.

Owls are found in all different habitats and there are different owl species found on all continents except Antarctica.

God made more than 220

kinds of owls.

Some of them are:

Saw-Whet owl

Great gray owl (the biggest—

33 inches tall)

Snowy owl

Barn owl

Great horned owl

Most owls live in trees, but burrowing owls actually live in underground burrows.

Many species of owls can live up to 20 years or more.

God made everything,

and he made it all good.

Just look around and something

special might just fly by!

CATS, DOGS, HAMSTERS, AND HORSES

About 62 percent of all households in the United States have a pet.

Studies show that people who have pets live longer, have less stress, and have fewer health problems.

God made all animals.

Some animals

have become friends for people.

One special animal pet is called a …

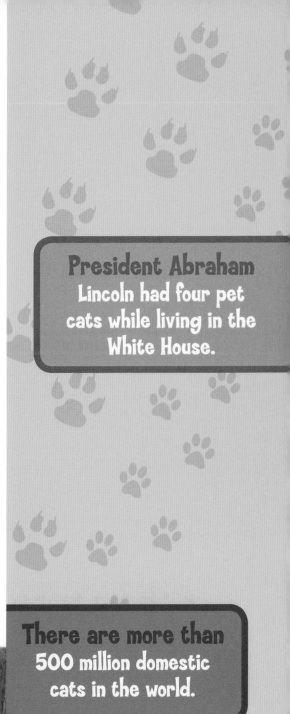

President Abraham Lincoln had four pet cats while living in the White House.

There are more than 500 million domestic cats in the world.

CAT!

A group of cats is called a clowder.

A male cat is called a tom.

God made about forty different kinds of cats.

Some are called Persian and Siamese.

Cats have different characteristics.

Persians have long, flowing coats and flat faces.

Siamese have creamy-colored short coats with darker ears, paws, and tails.

All cats have strong teeth and jaws, good hearing, and can see well in the dark.

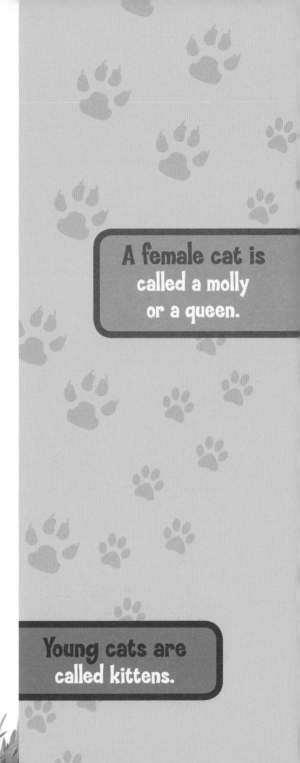

A female cat is called a molly or a queen.

Young cats are called kittens.

Most cats live ten to fifteen years.
To keep a cat happy and healthy
people feed them a good diet
with vitamins and minerals.
Cats like to drink water.
People think milk is a good drink
for cats. But be careful!
Many cats get sick
if they drink cow's milk.

Cats need doctor visits just like people. But cats help take care of themselves too. They clean their fur by licking. Cats use their tongues, which feel like sandpaper, to do this job.

Cats have excellent hearing and a great sense of smell.

Cats are considered natural hunters and will often stalk their prey.

People in Egypt and China believed that cats were sacred ... that means extra special.

An ailurophile is a person who loves cats.

Cats let people know how they feel.

When cats are happy, they purr.

When cats are upset, they hiss and can scratch.

If a cat gets nervous, you might see its tail or ears twitch.

Cats love to play.

Cats like yarn, bells, and catnip.

They also like to just be petted.

For short distances,
cats can run up to
30 miles an hour!

Cats spend up to
30% of their awake
time grooming.

It is said that dogs are probably the first animal that people tamed and trained.

A common nickname for the dog is "man's best friend."

God made all animals.

Some animals

have become friends for people.

One special animal pet is called a …

DOG!

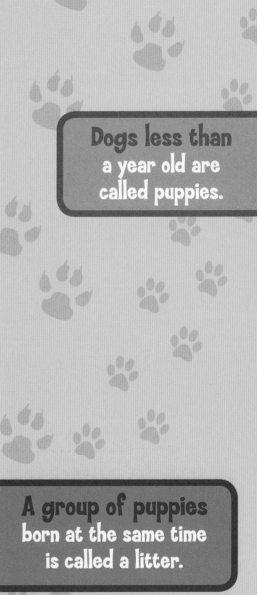

Dogs less than a year old are called puppies.

A group of puppies born at the same time is called a litter.

Many people have dogs as pets. God made many breeds of dogs— so many that it is difficult to count. Some kinds of dogs are Labradors and Chihuahuas.

A group of dogs is called a pack.

Studies show that the Labrador is the most popular breed of dog for families because of its friendly personality.

The largest dog in history is a Great Dane named Zeus who measured 44 inches tall.

Some dogs make good friends for families.

These dogs are taught to be gentle and behave well.

They can be protective and love to run and play.

Dogs can be as small as three pounds and as many as 175 pounds when full-grown.

Dogs can be trained to help people with hunting and farming.

It is said that dogs can hear sounds at more than four times the distance than humans.

Some dogs learn special skills.

They help people live safely

and do their jobs.

Some dogs help people who cannot

see or hear well.

Other dogs help police find

lost people or things.

People who have dogs feed them diets with vitamins and minerals. Some dogs love to share people food, but it is not always healthy!

On average, dogs live from 10-15 years.

Pet dogs are omnivores—that means they eat meat as well as vegetables and grain.

Based on a survey taken by vets in the United States, Max is the most popular dog name.

The fastest dog is the Greyhound who can run up to 40 miles per hour.

People can train their dogs to do tricks.

Some people take their dog to school.

But don't forget, dogs love to play too!

God made all animals.

Some animals

have become friends for people.

One special animal pet is called a …

HAMSTER!

It is believed that hamsters originated in the desert area of east Asia.

Most hamsters have thick fur and can be colored black, grey, brown, white, yellow, red, or a mix.

God made many kinds of hamsters.
Some hamsters that make
good pets are Dwarf, Teddy Bear,
and Panda hamsters.
These can all be found at pet shops
along with supplies they need
to stay healthy and safe.

A hamster is a kind of rodent, like the mouse, rat, and squirrel.

Hamsters often live for two to three years if they are well cared for and have plenty of food and water.

Most hamsters like to live in their cage alone.

Hamsters should have constant access to water—they get thirsty just like people.

Hamsters have poor eyesight.

Since many live in burrows,

it is fine for them.

Even if hamsters live in cages

they like to burrow under

torn-up paper and cardboard tubes.

Hamsters have good hearing, and

their noses work great too.

People keep their pet hamsters healthy with good food and fresh water. If they get sick, a veterinarian can care for a hamster.

These tiny animals have large pouches in their cheeks to store food like seeds and carry food back to their burrows or nests.

Hamsters can carry up to half their weight in their cheek pouches.

Hamsters are nocturnal, so they will be awake a lot at night, running on their exercise wheels.

To help a hamster stay healthy, people make sure the hamster has a clean cage and an exercise wheel for running. People even get clear exercise balls for their hamster to roll and ride in.

Hamsters have special feet that allow them to run forward and backward too.

Hamsters have large front teeth that keep growing.

They must have things to chew on, like hamster-safe sticks and even dog biscuits.

These help their teeth stay short.

Hamsters have 16 teeth that continuously grow.

God made all animals.

Some animals

have become friends for people.

One special animal pet is called a …

An adult male horse is called a stallion and a young male horse is called a colt.

HORSE!

An adult female horse is called a mare, and a young female horse is called a filly.

There are more than 300 breeds of horses in the world. God made every one! People had horses more than 3,000 years before Jesus was born. There are cave drawings and bones in museums to show us.

People used horses for work
and transportation long ago.
Farmers used horses to plow or ride.
Others used horses to pull carriages.
Today, people have horses for work
and enjoyment.

Some people train their horses to play games with people, like polo.

Many horses are raised and trained to run fast in horse races, like the Kentucky Derby.

People who have horses feed them

foods with vitamins and minerals,

like oats, hay, and special grains.

Some horses get treats

like sugar and apples.

Horses need lots of water every day.

Horses are herbivores—they eat only plants.

When a horse is moving we call it a gait.

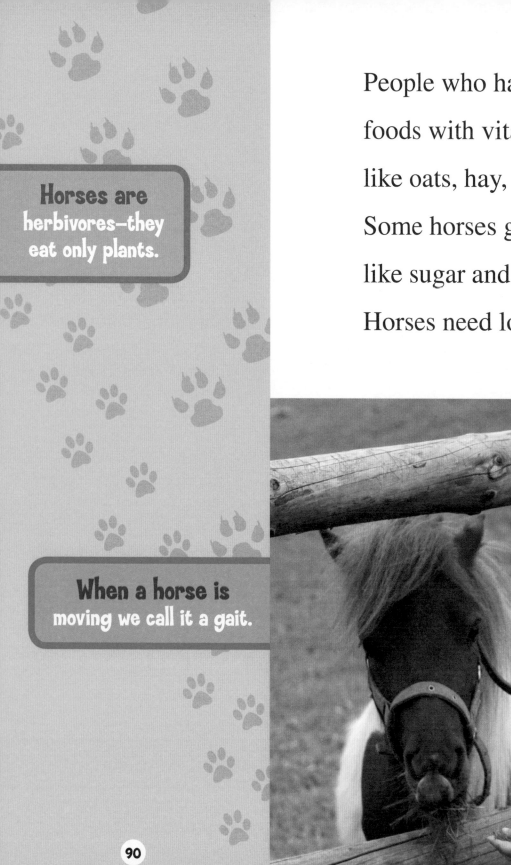

Horses let their owners know how they feel.

The way a horse moves its body can show whether it is happy, upset, or scared and startled.

Horses move in four basic gaits—walk, trot, cantor, and gallop.

Every gait has a different pattern determined by how many hooves leave the ground at a time.

A horse will be a happy pet as long as its owner cares for and loves it, grooms and feeds it, and makes sure it has plenty of exercise and rest.

BARNYARD CRITTERS

God made all creatures.

He made wild animals that live
in jungles.

He made tame animals too.

Some live in our homes.

Others live on farms
and are called livestock, like …

The five most
common farm
animals are:
chickens
cows
sheep
ducks
pigs

COWS!

The most common breeds of cow in North America are: Holstein-Friesian, Jersey, and Guernsey.

Cows drink about a bathtub full of water a day.

Cows live in herds.

Fathers are called bulls.

Mothers are called cows.

A heifer is a female cow that hasn't had a calf yet.

Cows came to America with the Pilgrims.

Baby cows are called calves.
Cows carry their babies for
nine months before giving birth.
A bull can grow up to weigh
an amazing 3,000 pounds!

Meat from cows is called beef.

Burgers and steaks are beef.

We use cowhides for leather

to make clothing, shoes, and belts.

Dairy cows are milked twice a day.

We drink milk and use it to make

cheese, yogurt, and ice cream!

One cow can produce 46,000 glasses of milk a year.

Cows are usually milked two or three times a day for a period of 10 months. Then they are usually given a break of several months.

We call cattle that work hard plowing or pulling wagons oxen.

We can also use cows to pull things on a farm, like plows and carts. We use their manure to help plants grow.

A cow chews her cud (regurgitated, partially digested food) for up to 8 hours each day.

Cattle do something gross!

They eat food, swallow it,

spit it back up, chew it,

and swallow it again.

This is called chewing their cud.

God made another animal on the farm

that chews their cud, the …

An average dairy cow eats about 40 pounds of feed a day.

GOAT!

Goats can live 10 to 15 years.

Goats have only bottom front and side teeth and their top jaw has a large back molar for crushing things.

Like cows, goats have special stomachs with four parts. Goats are curious. They like to taste everything but are fussy about what they eat.

Just like cows, goats chew their cud.

Goats are good climbers and are often seen standing on their back legs to reach leaves to eat.

Goats can weigh from 22 to 275 pounds depending on the breed of goat.

Goats were kept by sailors for their milk.

Goats come in many colors.

Most goats have horns, beards, and short hair.

Billy goats are smelly!

This is because of a spot on their head called a musk gland.

Goats live all over the world. People drink their milk, eat their meat, and use their hair and hide.

Cashmere is a type of material used for making clothes made from the wool of a special goat.

Goats are also great pets!

They are friendly and smart.

Goats can be trained to walk on a leash.

Goats live in groups called herds.

Goats can be trained to work as a pack animal —properly trained, a goat can carry up to 25% of its body weight.

Mother goats are called does or nannies.

Father goats are called bucks or billies.

Baby goats are called kids.

Mothers often give birth

to twins or triplets.

Goats are herbivores (plant-eaters) and do not really like food that is dirty or has been on the ground.

In the Old Testament, people in Jericho had goats for food and milk.

God made all farm animals,

and he made them all good, like the …

PIG!

The hippopotamus is the pig's distant cousin.

Ancient cave paintings show people from long ago hunting pigs.

Pigs have a snout for a nose,

and a small, curly or straight tail.

They have a big body and short legs.

Most pigs have four toes on each foot.

They walk on the two middle toes.

The other toes help them balance.

Pigs have sharp tusks that they use for digging and protection if they live the wild.

Farmers sometimes remove the tusks to help protect their workers and other pigs.

Pigs are clean animals.

They do not like to make a mess

where they eat or sleep.

But pigs do not sweat.

They cool off by rolling in water

or mud during the summer.

The mud helps a pig not get sunburn.

Mud also keeps away flies.

Pigs have poor eyesight but have a very good sense of smell.

Some people believe that pigs are the smartest domesticated animal— even smarter than the dog!

Pigs are omnivores.

They eat meat and plants.

Unlike cattle and goats,

pigs must chew their food well

the first time they eat it.

They have 44 teeth to help them.

Piglets weigh about
2 1/2 pounds at birth.

Adult pigs can weigh
from 300-700 pounds.

Mother pigs are called sows.

Father pigs are called boars.

Baby pigs are called piglets.

A group of piglets is called a litter.

Sows have 6–12 piglets in a litter.

Pig meat is called pork.

Bacon and ham are pork.

The rough hair of a pig

is used for brushes.

It has been said that every part

of a pig is useful but the "oink!"

114

God created farm animals

big and small.

Some have hair and

others have feathers, like the …

There are about two billion pigs in the world.

CHICKEN!

There are more chickens in the world than any other kind of bird.

A chicken can run up to nine miles per hour when it wants to.

There are dozens of chicken breeds such as the Dutch bantam, leghorn, and Rhode Island red.

Chickens are a kind of bird.

They are also called poultry.

There are thousands of kinds of

chickens all over the world!

Chickens provide eggs and meat to eat.

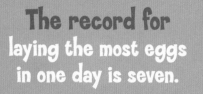

The record for laying the most eggs in one day is seven.

Chicken eggs come in colors other than white and brown. Some breeds lay eggs in shades of blue or green.

Mother chickens are called hens.

Father chickens are called roosters.

Chickens live in groups called flocks.

Babies are called chicks.

Hens sit on their eggs until they hatch after 21 days.

Chickens have a red crest of skin
on their heads called a comb.
On their chins are red wattles,
which help keep them cool.
Roosters have sharp spurs
on their heels for fighting.

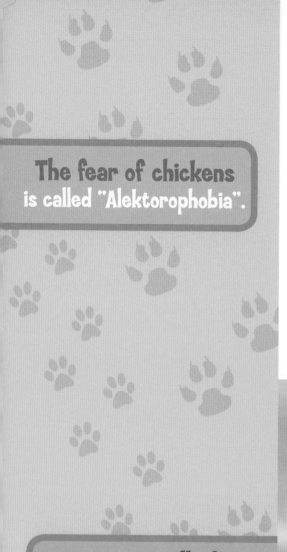

Chicken feathers are many amazing colors and patterns.

Like pigs, chickens are omnivores.

They can catch and eat mice.

They scratch at the ground to look for plants, seeds, and bugs to eat.

Chickens live in houses called coops.
Coops protect them at night
when other animals, like red foxes,
raccoons, and coyotes, hunt them.
Coops have boxes to lay eggs in
and roosts to stand on.

Chickens don't
have teeth.

Fertilized chicken eggs
usually take 21 days
to hatch.

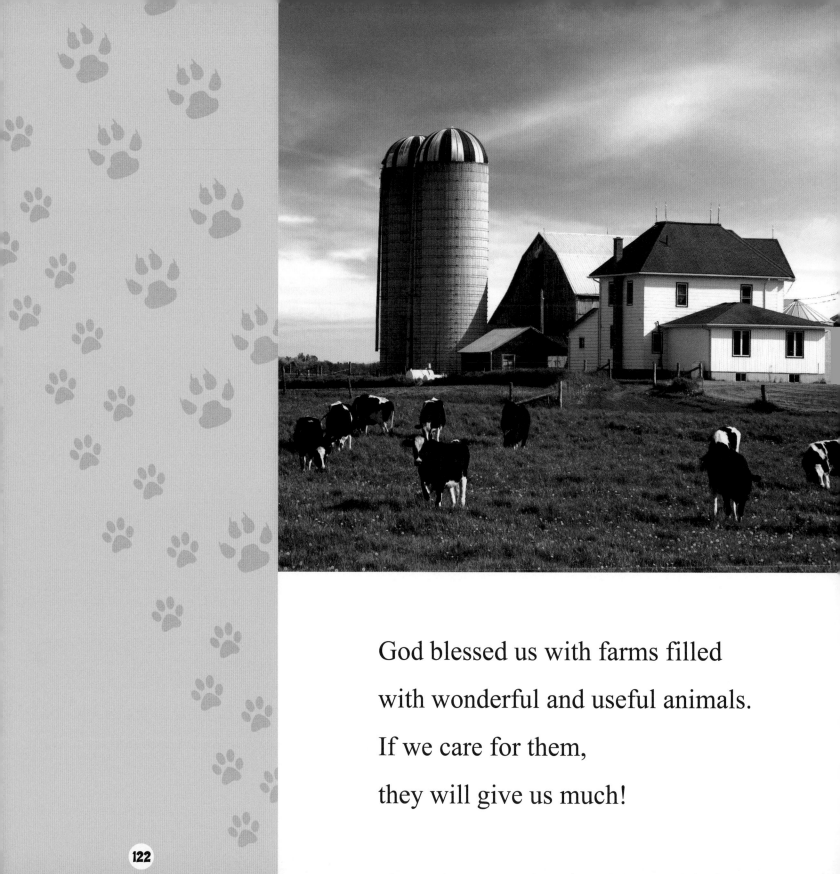

God blessed us with farms filled

with wonderful and useful animals.

If we care for them,

they will give us much!

Taurophobia is the fear of bulls.

Scientists believe that the closest living relative to the Tyrannosaurus Rex is the chicken.

Horses can live up to 30 years!

Subject Index

If you love *Animals All Around*, you'll love

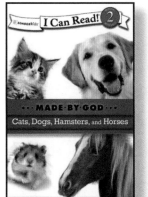

these other books about God's creation!

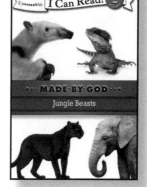

I Can Read! 2 — MADE BY GOD — Big Bugs, Little Bugs

I Can Read! 2 — MADE BY GOD — Curious Creatures Down Under

I Can Read! 2 — MADE BY GOD — Polar Pals

I Can Read! 2 — MADE BY GOD — Barnyard Critters

I Can Read! 2 — MADE BY GOD — Forest Friends

I Can Read! 2 — MADE BY GOD — Jungle Beasts

Come explore God's creation with *Nature of God.*

Available in stores and online!

ZONDERkidz
.com